Bad ~~New~~ Girl in Town

James A. Madison High School
Monday, 7:57 am

B-R-N-N-N-N-G!
WE GET MORE RINGS THAN A BATH TUB!
=groan=
WORST.
PUN.
EVER.
*
Prayer Club

SCOPE THE NEW TASSEL WITH BLUE HAIR.
OFFICE
LIBRARY

I'M SURE WE'LL MEET HER SOON ENOUGH.
WONDER WHAT SHE'S LIKE?
HARPER, Serenity
I BELIEVE EVERY PUPIL DESERVES AN OPPORTUNITY, MISS HARPER, BUT --
-- YOU ALREADY BLEW YOUR SECOND, THIRD, AND FOURTH CHANCES!
ONE MORE AND YOU'RE OUT!
THEN LET'S SPEED THINGS UP. CRAM IT --

DON'T TRY GETTING EXPELLED ON YOUR FIRST DAY!
WE'LL MAKE AN EFFORT -- BUT YOU MUST, TOO!
STUPID SCHOOL!
RINCIPAL
BUNCHA @#$+& DORKS...
LOOKS LIKE THE NEW GIRL CAN USE SOME HELP.

LOST?
I'M DEREK, THIS IS KIMBERLY AND TIM.

Prayer Club

"PRAYER CLUB?" OH, NO!
NOT BIBLE BANGERS!

I WANT NO HOLY ROLLER FRADOS DOGGING ME!

GOT A REP TO MAINTAIN!
DAWGZ, WE BEEN DISSED...
Prayer Club

DEREK LOOKS MIGHTY FINE.
Prayer Club

Y'KNOW, IT JUST MIGHT BE FUN --
-- TO REEL IN A CHOIR BOY!
CLASS, WELCOME SERENITY HARPER FROM LOS ANGELES.
JUST SHOOT ME . . .

SURE ISN'T WINNING FRIENDS . . .

HEY! YOU!

WATCH YOURSELF, CHIPPER!
WE'VE GOT SCHOOL SPIRIT HERE!

THAT'S ALL YOU'VE GOT, SKOOCHIE!

YOU WANT DRAMA --
-- I'LL PUT THE SMACK DOWN ON YA!

=gnrrrrrr!=

LOSERS!

WHOA! DON'T GET IN TROUBLE BECAUSE SHE'S AN IDIOT!

ext morning...

SERENITY FITS IN LIKE A TARANTULA ON A WEDDING CAKE.

SHE MUST FEEL LONELY.
GOT A FUNNY WAY OF MAKING FRIENDS ...

INCLUDE HER IN OUR PRAYERS ...
... AND MAKE AN EFFORT TO WELCOME HER ...

SHE'S HANGING WITH THE WORST CROWD IN SCHOOL!
MAYBE 'CUZ NOBODY ELSE WILL HANG WITH HER.
YO! SERENITY!
LET'S TALK TO HER.
WHY IS HE SO INTERESTED IN HELPING HER?

WANT TO COME TO OUR YOUTH GROUP TONIGHT?
YOU UP WITH THEM? GOTTA BE A SNITCH!
DAWGZ!

YOU AND YOUR @#$+& BIBLES!
WHOOPS!
Can't show that in a Christian manga!

THERE GOES ONE GIRL WITH ISSUES!
=rant!=
=rave!=
=snort!=
SHE'S SET THE WORLD REC
IN RUDE!
SHE'S BEYOND HELP! FLUSH HER.
WHAT? GOT SOMETHING TO ADD?
JUST GLA
GOD WON'
FLUSH US
NO MATTER HO
UNLOVABLE
WE ACT..

I HATE IT WHEN YOU'RE RIGHT.
?
BAD NEWS, SERENITY. YOU'RE REALLY GOING TO HATE THIS.
YOU ARE OUR NEW PET PROJECT!
NO MATTER HOW OBNOXIOUS YOU ACT --

-- NO MATTER HOW CRUDE YOU TALK --

-- WE'LL STILL BE YOUR FRIENDS.

THAT DOESN'T MEAN WE'LL TOLERATE RUDE BEHAVIOR OR WRONG DOING.
SCREW UP, WE'LL LET YOU KNOW ABOUT IT.
BUT IF YOU NEED HELP . . .
. . . OR SOMEBODY TO TALK TO . . .
. . . WE'LL BE THERE.

ang
ang
ang
BEAT PRESTON
WHY ME ?
WHY ME ?
WHY ME ?
SO WHICH IS IT ?
"SELF-INFLICTED" OR "RELIGIOUS PERSECUTION ?"
JUST GIMME THE ASPIRIN ...

OW!
@#$+&
THE ANGRY DEAD
chapt
2

@#$+&, IT'S NOT FUNNY!
IT IS WHEN IT HAPPENS TO YOU!
CUSSIN' WON'T MAKE IT FEEL BETTER.
WELL, IT @#$+& HURTS!
SHUT THE @#$+& UP!

WRITING THIS POETRY ASSIGNMENT WAS HARD!
ASK M IF I CARE.
CLASS, I REALLY MUST COMMEND YOU! SOME OF YOU WROTE OUTSTANDING POEMS!

"INCOMPLETE ?!?!?"
I WROTE A @#$+t POEM!
YOU WROTE A DIRTY LIMERICK.
Incomplete
YOU AID WRITE WHAT I FEEL --
Incomplete
-- THAT'S WHAT I @#$+t FEEL!
YOU'RE CENSORING ME!
ON THE CONTRARY, I'M TRYING TO LIBERATE YOU!

LISTEN HOW MORE COLORFUL THE BARD'S VOCABULARY SOUNDS.
THERE'S NOTHING YOU CAN SAY THAT SHAKESPEARE HASN'T ALREADY SAID MORE POETICALLY.
I GOT YOUR SHAKESPEARE RIGHT HERE . . .
DETENTION, MISS HARPER!
I'M GOING, I'M GOING!
!

CHILD, WHAT HAPPENED IN THERE?
WHADDYA THINK HAPPENED?
THAT OLD @#$+& HATES ME!
I AGREE.

HUH? YOU DO?

MS BAXTE
MR. PYLE IS HOPELESSLY MIRED IN OUTDATED EUROCENTRIC MASCULINE PRECEPTS!

. . . UH . . . YEAH . . .
SIT. PLEASE.
I HAVE NO IDEA WHAT SHE'S TALKING ABOUT!
HE MUSTN'T IMPOSE OBSOLETE PATRIARCHAL JUDEO-CHRISTIAN VALUES ON YOUNG WOMYN. *
* Note spellin
RESIST THEIR EFFORTS -- EMBRACE FREEDOM!
YEAH! FREEDOM! THAT'S ME!

ESCAPED DETENTION ALREADY ?
DIDN'T GO.
I TALKED TO MS BAXTER INSTEAD.
HEY, SERENITY, DON'T LET THE PYLE-DRIVER GET YOU DOWN.
... UH-OH ...

MS BAXTER
=oof=
SAID HE WAS
=ungh=
WRONG TO
CENSOR ME.
=grunt!=

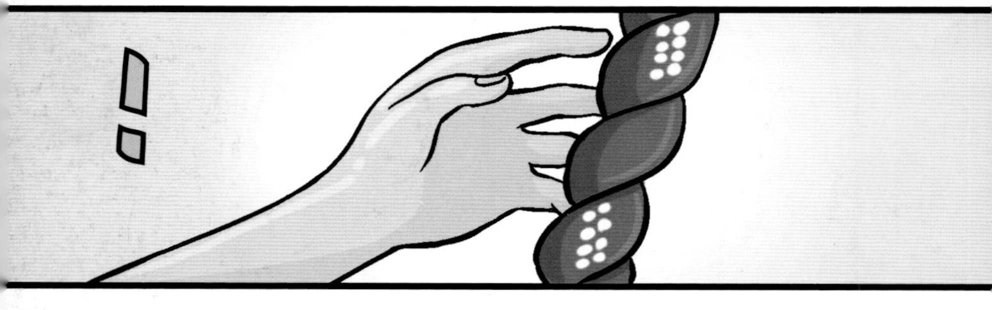
!

Y!!!!!!

OW

WHY HOLD MYSELF IN JUST TO MAKE SOMEBODY ELSE HAPPY?
WE CONSIDER OTHERS BEFORE WE SAY ANYTHING.
CHRISTIANS GO @#$+& IF SOMEBODY SAYS "POOPIE!"
I THINK "POOPIE" SOUNDS CUTE ...

Next morning...
MAYBE SHE'S GOT A POINT. WHY IS BAD LANGUAGE "BAD ?"
GRANTED, SAY "GOD" OR "JESUS" TOO MUCH ...
...YOU END UP TRIVIALIZING THEM.
THE N-WORD IS PRETTY AWFUL !
BUT IT ISN'T OBSCENE.

THAT'S THE PROBLEM -- NOT ANY ONE WORD, BUT THE CUMULATIVE EFFECT.
CASUAL BLASPHEMY TODAY MAKES IT EASIER TO IGNORE GOD TOMORROW.
CHRISTIANS SHOULD SPEAK BOLDLY AND FRANKLY ...
... BUT ALWAYS WITH LOVE.

OW!
GIMM
MY
MON
BAC
BAM-BAM-BAM
BAM
THAT DOES IT! I'M TALKING TO HER!

SERENITY! CUSSING WON'T HELP --
YOU!

CHRISTIANS ARE TOO MOLDY FOR ANYTHING STRONGER THAN "GOD BLESS!"

YOU THINK YOU @#$+t CUSS?
@#$+t
COUNTER-ROTATING
@#$+t
PERPENDICULAR
@#$+t
=klunk!=
SEE, WE DON'T TRASH TALK CUZ IT ISN'T DECK.
...UH... YEAH...
WHERE DID YOU LEARN THAT?
MY UNCLE'S A MARINE DRILL INSTRUCTOR.
MAGGOTS!

Later...
WRONG AGAIN, MISS HARPER!
x 3(x²) =42
OH, F--
x²) =42
. . . . .
...FIDGET...

chapt 3
WHAT !?!?!
IN SCHOOL ONE WEEK AND ALREADY SIX NOTES FROM YOUR PRINCIPAL !?!?!
HEY, MOM, I'M TRYIN' TO CONCENTRATE!

THEY'LL JAIL YOU AGAIN --
I AM IN JAIL -- YOU'RE THE WARDEN!

COME BACK HERE! WHERE DO YOU THINK YOU'RE GOING?
OUT!

SLam
=click=

" =click?= "
OH, NO!

MORON -- YOU JUST LOCKED YOURSELF OUT!

NO KEYS, NO MONEY!

IT'S FREEZIN'! * BUT I CAN'T GO BACK --
* Actually, only 68°

MOM WOULD HAVE TO LET ME IN. I DON'T WANT HER GLOATING!

CAN'T GO ANYWHERE . . . GOT NO FRIENDS . . . CAN'T GO BACK . . .
HUH, KIMBERLY'S CHURCH . . .

YOUTH GROUP TONITE

I DON'T WANNA GO . . . BUT THEY DID INVITE ME . . . AND IT'S WARM!

NAH -- WHY HANG WITH A BUNCHA BIBLE BANGING LOSERS?

'SIDES, I'M NOT DRESSED -- THEY'D LAUGH AT ME. OR GET OFFENDED . .

THAT'S IT! IF I TICK 'EM OFF --

-- THEY'LL NEVER BUG ME AGAIN !
IN FIRST CORINTHIANS, PAUL WROTE ON MARRIAGE AND DIVORCE --

YO ! YOUTH GROUP ?
WELCOME. YOU'RE SERENITY, RIGHT ?
MY DAUGHTER KIMBERLY MENTIONED A NEW GIRL.

I'M PASTOR CALVIN.
. . . . .
WHERE'S YOUR BIBLE?
DON'T OWN ONE.
NO BIBLE? WE CAN'T HAVE THAT! HERE, TAKE THIS ONE.
IN CORINTHIANS . . .
WHAT'S A "CORINTHIANS?"
TRY THE NEW TESTAMENT.
WHAT'S A "TESTAMENT?"

PAUL REPEATS CHRIST'S ADMONITION AGAINST DIVORCE.
HUH?

WHY SHOULDN'T PEOPLE GET DIVORCED? WHY HANG AROUND AND BE MISERABLE?

DIVORCE USUALLY HARMS CHILDREN.
MY PARENTS DIVORCED AND I'M OKAY!

WHAT ?!?!?!
=KOFF= =KOFF=
... MRRR...

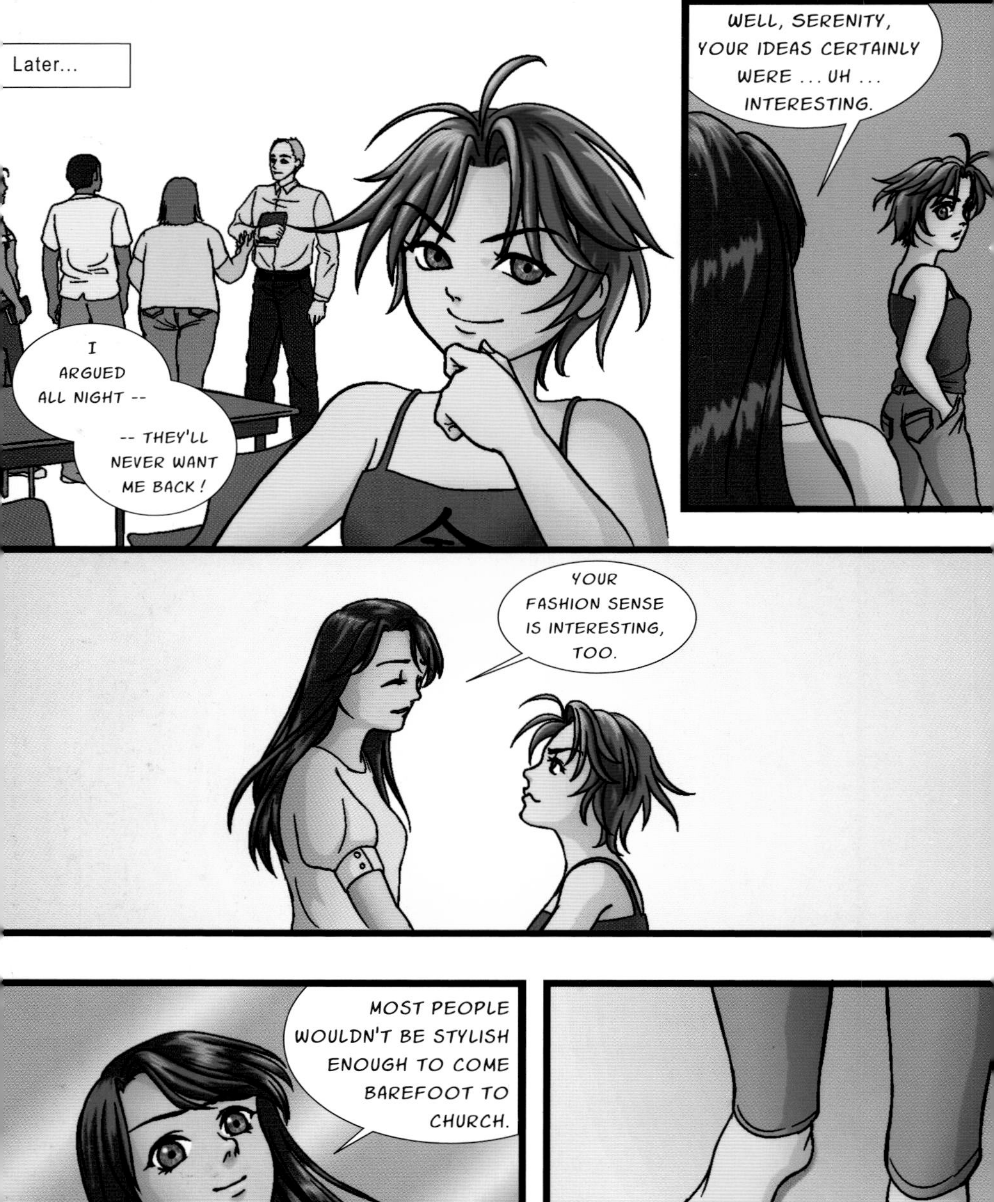
Later...
I ARGUED ALL NIGHT --
-- THEY'LL NEVER WANT ME BACK!
WELL, SERENITY, YOUR IDEAS CERTAINLY WERE ... UH ... INTERESTING.
YOUR FASHION SENSE IS INTERESTING, TOO.

MOST PEOPLE WOULDN'T BE STYLISH ENOUGH TO COME BAREFOOT TO CHURCH.
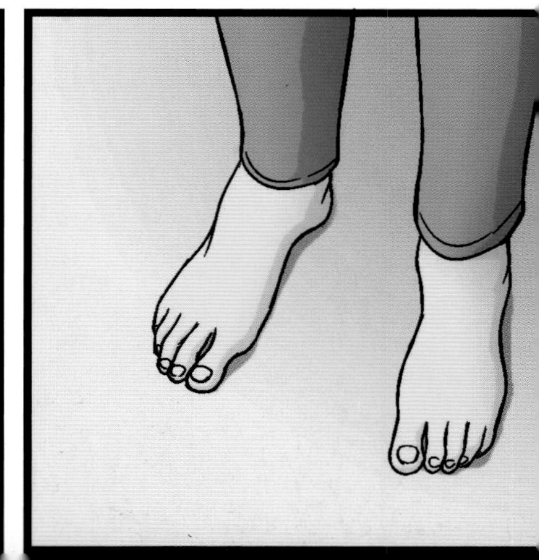

I LOCKED MYSELF OUT WITH NO SHOES.
HOW WILL YOU GET HOME?

WE'LL GIVE YOU A RIDE.
MAYBE DEREK CAN GIVE ME A RIDE.

WELL, IF DEREK --
I INSIST, DAD!
?

GOD LOVES YOU AS YOU ARE.
YOU MUST HATE MY ARGUING.

HE JUST WANTS YOUR FULL POTENTIAL.
SOUNDS LIKE MOM'S NEW AGE CRAP.

MANY NEW AGE BELIEFS ARE CHRISTIAN IDEALS DILUTED OF ALL MORAL AUTHORITY.

WHO NEEDS AUTHORITY? NO LIMITS! THAT'S WHAT I SAY!
GREAT! THEN YOU'LL WANT TO BE A CHRISTIAN!
???
CHRIST FREED US FROM SIN. HE DOESN'T CLOSE DOORS, HE OPENS THEM!

WHAT-EH-VAH!
AS LONG AS YOU'RE WILLING TO LISTEN, THERE'S HOPE.

"HOPE?"

MY LIFE'S A JOKE THAT I'M NOT IN ON.
NOBODY CARES!

GOD CARES.

THAT'S THE BIGGEST JOKE OF ALL.

SEE YOU NEXT WEEK?
I'LL THINK ABOUT IT.

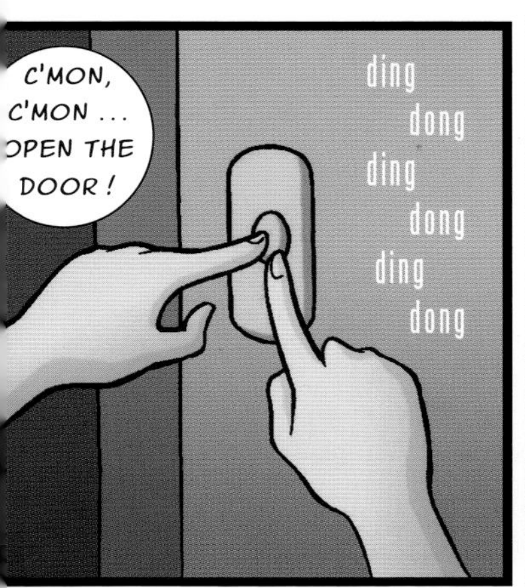
C'MON, C'MON ... OPEN THE DOOR!
ding dong ding dong ding dong

WHERE HAVE YOU BEEN?

IF OU MUST KNOW ...

... I WENT TO CHURCH!

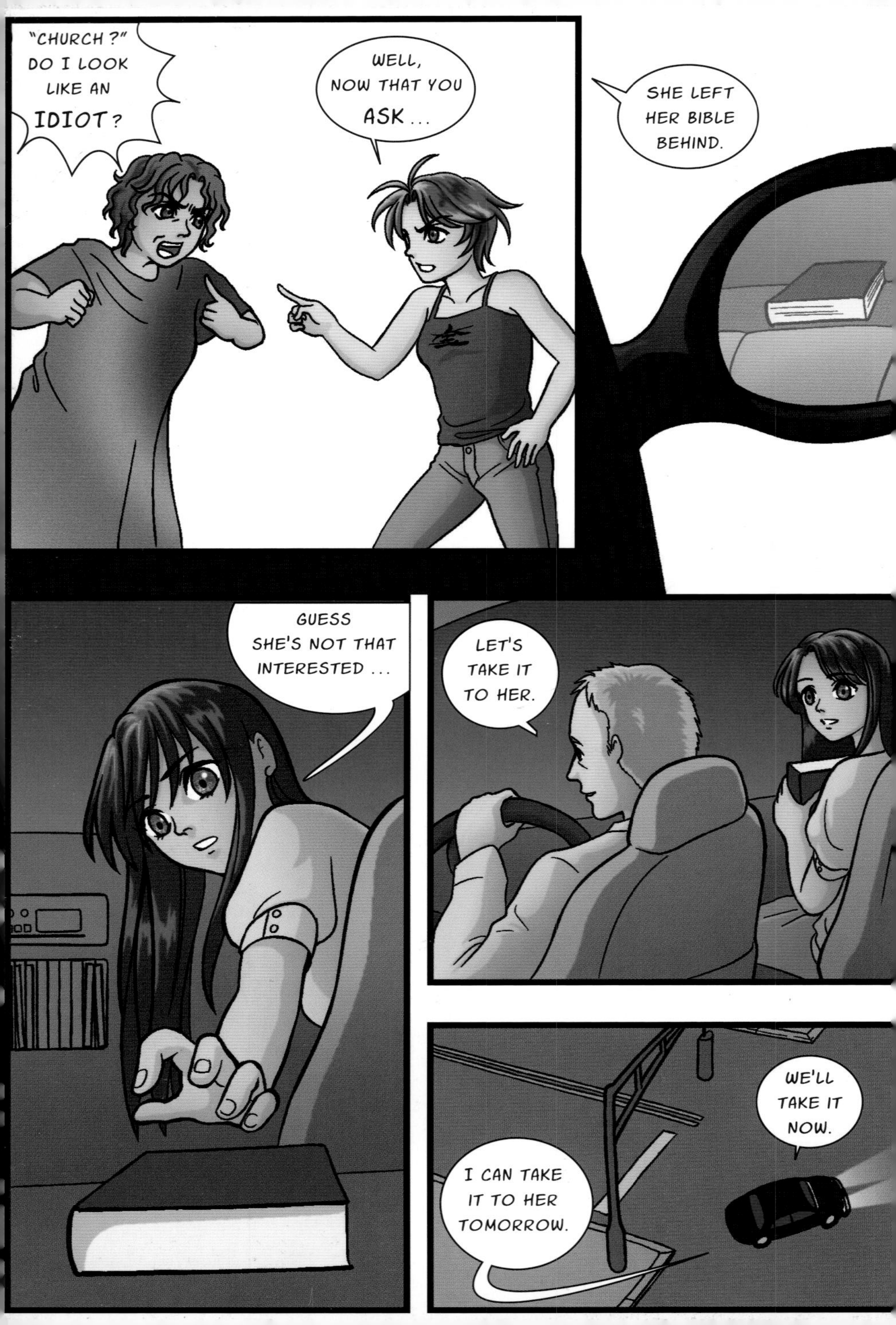
"CHURCH?" DO I LOOK LIKE AN IDIOT?
WELL, NOW THAT YOU ASK...
SHE LEFT HER BIBLE BEHIND.
GUESS SHE'S NOT THAT INTERESTED...
LET'S TAKE IT TO HER.
I CAN TAKE IT TO HER TOMORROW.
WE'LL TAKE IT NOW.

OU NEVER
RUST ME !
YOU LIE ALL THE TIME !
ding dong
YEAH ?
HI. I'M PASTOR CALVIN.
RENITY
SEE YOU NEXT WEEK ?
YEAH, MAYBE.
Y'KNOW, MAYBE I'LL GO --
-- JUST TO BUG MY MOTHER !

chap

4

CUTE, SALLY. YOUR IDEA?
A PUN THAT BAD? OF COURSE IT IS!
Preserve Wildlife - -
PICKLE A SQUIRREL!

OLLECTING FOR YOUR CHURCH?
NAH. THIS IS FOR THE ANIMAL SHELTER.
YOU HAVE ANY PETS?
YEAH, TINKERBELLE. SHE'S AN ARIZONA --

BRNNNG!
= GROAN! = ANOTHER FIRE DRILL!
ALL CLASSES, THIS IS A DRILL. GO TO YOUR ASSIGNED LOCATIONS.
WORRY ABOUT THAT LATER, SALLY. FALL IN FOR THE DRILL.
HEY!

WHERE DID MY MONEY GO!?!?!
PRINCIPAL PARK
HOW MUCH WAS IN YOUR JAR?
FIFTEEN BUCKS, MAYBE MORE. IT WASN'T MINE -- IT WAS THE SHELTER'S!
WHO WAS WITH YOU?
SERENITY HARPER.
Serenity Harper
WHY AM I NOT SURPRISED?

HOW COME I ALWAYS GET BLAMED FOR SOMETHING?
YOUR REPUTATION PRECEDES YOU!
THAT DOESN'T MEAN I'M A THIEF! GO AHEAD, SEARCH MY LOCKER!
I DID! YOU'RE LUCKY I FOUND NOTHING -- OTHERWISE YOU'D BE ARRESTED!

THERE'S THAT SKANK, SERENITY!
I HEAR SHE'S A THIEF! WHO NEEDS HER?

SERENITY IS A LOGICAL SUSPECT.
GIVE HER THE BENEFIT OF A DOUBT.
??? WHY IS DEREK DEFENDING SERENITY?
SERENITY BETTER NOT HAVE TAKEN IT!
PRAY GOD KEEPS OUR HEARTS --
-- AND EYES AND MINDS -- OPEN!
. . . . .

WE ACCEPT YOUR STORY -- THIS TIME !
DON'T DO ME ANY FAVORS !
WE'RE NOT ! YOU CAN FOOL PEOPLE BUT NOT GOD !
WHAT-E-VAH !
I ALMOST WISH SHE IS GUILTY ! SHE'D BE EXPELLED AND OUTTA HERE !

WHY ARE YOU TURNING SERENITY FROM A PROJECT INTO A CAREER?
HMMM, KIMBERLY KEEPS DEREK ON A TIGHT LEASH!
HE MAY WANNA ROAM!
HOOKING UP WITH HIM MAY BE EASIER THAN I THOUGHT!

Serenity --
Make sure
you
CHIPS

TTER
BRIGHT
SUGAR
BRIGHTLY COLORED
SUGAR JUNK
AUTHORIZED
PERSONNEL
ONLY
KNOCK
FIRST
STUPID!

HEY, TINKERBELLE ! HOW'S MY GIRL ?
THE GERUNDING
THE ANGRY DEAD
FASHION
FASHION
YouBET I am...
...AnTiSociaL!
BOOYAH !
The ANGRY DEAD are on their Suffer And Die Tour !

I NEED ANOTHER ADVANCE ON MY LLOWANCE!
TOUGH, KID. I'M TAPPED OUT.
YOU DON'T UNDERSTAND -- YOU NEVER UNDERSTAND!
I UNDERSTAND YOU'RE IN TROUBLE!
PRINCIPAL PARKER E-MAILED ME!
WHATEVER SHE SAID ABOUT ME IS A LIE!

SHE SAID SOMETHING ABOUT MISSING MONEY !
SERENIT
IF YOU'R
STEALIN
AGAIN -
NOBODY CARES ABOUT ME !

THAT MAKES TWO OF US!
I WISH I WAS DEAD!
=SOB= waiiiiiiiil!
AUTHORIZED PERSONNEL ONLY
KNOCK FIRST STUPID!
SLAM!
Boo-Hoo-Hoo!
THERE -- THAT SHOULD GIVE HER THE GUILTS!

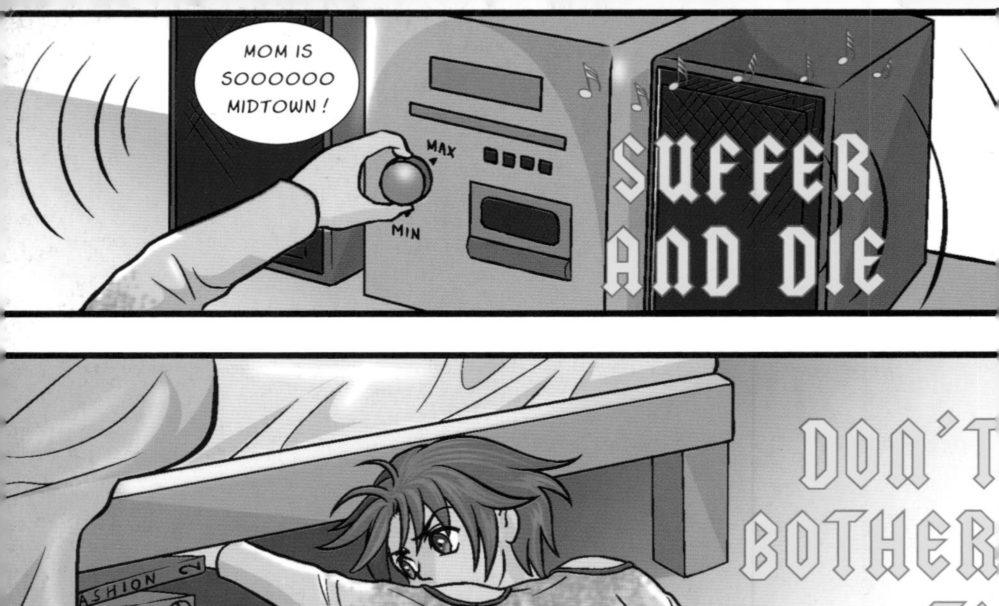
MOM IS SOOOOOO MIDTOWN!
MAX
MIN
SUFFER AND DIE

DON'T BOTHER TO CRY
I CAN'T BELIEVE SHE WAS A HIPPIE.

JUST SUFFER AND DIE
NO ALLOWANCE? NO PROBLEM!

HA!
THEY THOUGHT
THEY COULD KEEP
THEIR TREASURE SAFE!
THEY WERE
WRONG!
ANOTHER
UCCESSFUL
RAID BY
ERENITY
CROFT!
©+TM *
* Just kidding! Please don't sue us!
WADY ...?

...WHY DO YOU WANNA WOB US...?
HEY, NOTHING PERSONAL.
I'M FROM A DYSFUNCTIONAL FAMILY.
YOU CAN'T BLAME ME.
CAN YOU?

SHION 6
chapt
5

THE GERUNDING
I DON'T BELIEVE THAT FAIRY TALE ABOUT GOD SEEING EVERYTHING!
THAT'S STUPID!
LIKE BELIEVING IN SANTA CLAUS OR THE EASTER BUNNY!

I FEEL TERRIBLE. COULDN'T SLEEP LAST NIGHT ...WEIRD DREAMS...
YOU LOOK TERRIBLE.
SUGARJUNK

I'VE GOT TO WORK LATE TONIGHT.
THINK
'OU CAN
Y OUT OF
OUBLE?

CAN YOU STAY OUT OF TROUBLE ?!?!?
YEAH! SURE! OKAY!

DEREK, THE PRAYER CLUB SAID IF I NEEDED HELP TO ASK . . .
I'M FLUNKING ALGEBRA. COULD YOU HELP ME THIS AFTERNOON ?
I PROMISED KIMBERLY . . .
OH.
I UNDERSTAND.
I THOUGHT YOU MEANT IT WHEN . . .
NEVER MIND . . .
UH . . . IS IT OKAY WITH YOUR MOM IF I COME BY ?

OH, IT WAS HER IDEA.
YOU CAN ASK HER WHEN YOU COME.
BUT IF YOU CAN'T MAKE IT . . .
WELL . . . IF IT'S TO HELP YOU . . .
GOTCHA !

DEREK MAY BE A CHRISTIAN --
-- BUT HE'S STILL A BOY --
-- AND WHEN SERENITY HARPER WANTS A BOY --
-- SHE NAILS HIM!

SCORE ONE FOR THE HOME TEAM, OH, YEAH!
'COURSE, DEREK IS SO CLUELESS HE MIGHT NOT CARRY PROTECTION --
-- BUT MS BAXTER GAVE ME SOME SO HE WON'T HAVE THAT EXCUSE!
ding dong
SHOWTIME!

HI, DEREK . . .
HI.
. . . UH . . .
YOU CHANGED . . .
YEAH. THIS FEELS MORE COMFORTABLE!
Y'KNOW... LOOSER . . .
CLICK
WHERE'S YOUR MOM?

SHE ALLED.
SHE'S WORKING LATE.
REAL TE ...
C'MON, SIT. WHAT ARE YOU AFRAID WILL HAPPEN?
I'M NOT AFRAID OF ANYTHING HAPPENING ...
??? WHERE'S OUR ALGEBRA BOOK?
... MUSTA FORGOT IT ...

LOOK, I BETTER GO...
HEY! YOU JUST GOT HERE!
AFRAID KIMBERL MIGHT SA SOMETHING

NO, 'CUZ NOTHING'S GONNA HAPPEN SHE MIGHT HAVE SOMETHING TO SAY ABOUT!

IF I COULD FIGURE THAT OUT, I WOULDN'T NEED HELP IN ALGEBRA!

I'LL SPELL IT OUT. "SEE YA."
SHE'LL NEVER KNOW! WHAT'S THE HARM?

WHAT IF YOUR BOYFRIEND CHEATED ON YOU?
IT HAPPENED! I DIDN'T WHINE!
NOW YOU'RE "GETTING EVEN" BY HURTING INNOCENT PEOPLE?
THAT MAKES NO SENSE.

WHY NOT CLIMB A TOWER AND START SHOOTING?

I THOUGHT ABOUT IT!

LOSER !
VROOOOOOOM!
. . . SLUT . . .

HOW COULD I HAVE BEEN SO STUPID?
HE HATES ME NOW!
FASHION
FASHION
HE'S GONNA TELL EVERYBODY AT SCHOOL I'M A SKANK!
NOBODY WILL EVER LOVE ME!
EVEN DEREK COULDN'T STAND ME TOUCHING HIM!
33° Fahrenheit

6
WHAT HAPPENED YESTERDAY?
WHY DID YOU CANCEL OUT?
MIL LEN NIA
SOMETHING CAME UP.
NOTHING I WANT TO TALK ABOUT...
WHY? WHAT HAPPENED

THFULLY NESTLY, THING PPENED --
-- SO LET'S LEAVE IT AT THAT!
SOMETHING DID HAPPEN -- I KNOW IT!
YET . . . DEREK'S NEVER LIED TO ME.
SHOULDN'T I TRUST HIM?
DOESN'T HE DESERVE THE BENEFIT OF A DOUBT?

MAYBE I CAN'T PROVE ANYTHING . . .
. . . AND MAYBE NOTHING HAPPENED . . .
. . . BUT SOMETHING IS GOING ON !

UH, DEREK, CAN WE TALK . . . ?
NOTHING TO TALK ABOUT. NOTHING HAPPENED.

. . . UH, LOOK . . .

I'LL UNDERSTAND IF YOU DON'T WANT ME AROUND ANYMORE . . .

AT LEAST LET ME GET AWAY FROM YOU JESUS FREAKS !
NO, YOU CAN HANG AROUND. THE PRAYER CLUB IS ALWAYS OPEN.

AND I'LL WELCOME YOU AS A FRIEND ... NOTHING MORE, NOTHING LESS!

THIS ISN'T CHRISTIAN, BUT --
-- IF SERENITY WANTS DEREK, SHE'S GOT A WAR!

SEVENTEEN LOUSY DOLLARS AND THIRTY-SEVEN CENTS.
TAKE IT AND SPEND IT!
ON WHAT? SOME STUPID CD AND A STALE PIZZA?
BIG DEAL.
THE G
SQANCO
WELL, WHAT DID SALLY EVER DO FOR ME?
BESIDES BEING NICE?
THE GERUNDING
SQANCO

LEAVE IT AT KIMBERLY'S CHURCH. THEY'LL DONATE IT TO CHARITY.

YEAH, BUT PEOPLE GAVE THIS MONEY TO THE ANIMAL SHELTER.
IS IT STILL STEALING IF I GIVE THE MONEY TO SOMEBODY ELSE ?
SEVENTEEN DOLLARS AND THIRTY-SEVEN CENTS - -
- - WHAT COULD THEY GET WITH THAT ?
WHATEVER, IT'LL MEAN MOR
TO THEM THAN A COLD PIZZ
TO ME !

I WON'T GET ANY SLEEP UNTIL I RESOLVE THIS, SO . . .
. . . TAKE IT BACK.

PRINCIPAL PARKER
HEY! WHO'S IN THERE?
COME OUT OR I'LL CALL THE COPS!
PRINCIPAL P

SO FAR,
SO GOOD . . .
!

SLAM!

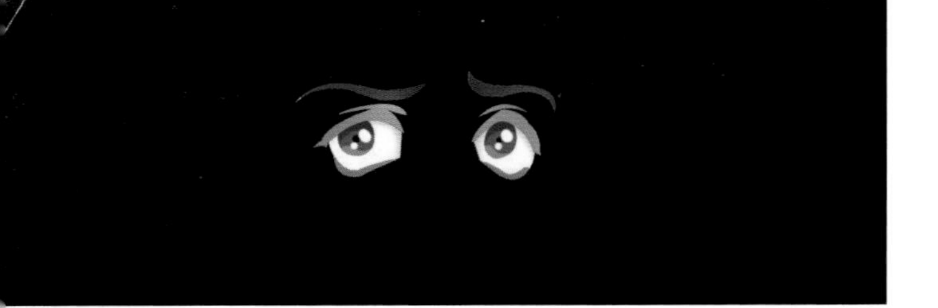

BACK THIS WAY, OFFICER. I HEARD HIM JUMP ON THE DUMPSTER!

YIKES! BETTER STAY HIDDEN UNTIL THEY LEAVE . . .

HE COULDN'T HAVE GOTTEN FAR!

. . . THEN I CAN SNEAK HOME . . . . . . SHOWER . . . SLEEP . . .
snzzzzzzzzzzzz

PLOP!
HUH? WUZZAT?

OH, NO! FELL ASLEEP! I GOTTA GET OUTTA HERE!
YOU THINK THE TRESPASSER MAY STILL BE HIDING?
IF I'M CAUGHT, T'S JAIL FOR SURE -- NO PROBATION THIS TIME!
WHAT'LL I DO? WHAT'LL I DO? WHAT'LL I DO?
Garbage fingers -- YUCK !!!

THE PRAYER CLUB MY ONLY CHANCE!
UH, HI. YOU SAID I COULD COME BY...
OUR DOOR IS ALWAYS OPEN.
I JUST WISH THE WINDOW WAS!

THANKS!
PE-HEW!
FEH!
WOTTA STINK!
WHA --!
HOW DID THAT GET HERE?
SEND SALLY RICHMOND TO MY OFFICE!
INTERCOM

SOMEBODY RETURNED YOUR MONEY.
ARE YOU STILL GOING TO INVESTIGATE ?
I SHOULD . . .
. . . BUT I WON'T. I THINK THE THIEF ALREADY PUNISHED HERSELF.
WHAT'S WITH SERENITY ?
YOU ASK ME, SHE'S SMELLING LIKE A ROSE !

WHAT'S THE REALBUZZ?

REALBUZZ STUDIOS IS AN INTERNATIONAL GROUP OF ARTISTS AND WRITERS CREATING EXCITING AND ENTERTAINING ORIGINAL STORIES FOR INSPIRATIONAL AND CHRISTIAN READERS.

WE RIDE THE CUTTING EDGE OF THE NEW BLEND OF AMERICAN AND ASIAN TALENT IN BREAKOUT CONTEMPORARY MEDIA.

SERENITY IS JUST THE FIRST OF MANY EXCITING NEW CHARACTERS AND STORIES COMING SOON FROM REALBUZZ STUDIOS. FROM THE ANCIENT PAST TO THE FAR FUTURE, FROM AROUND THE WORLD TO JUST AROUND THE CORNER, REALBUZZ STUDIOS BRINGS A SPECIAL MIX OF STYLISH, FUN, UPLIFTING STORIES JUST FOR YOU!

STICK AROUND --
WE'RE JUST GETTIN' STARTED!

Chapter

THERE'S A REASON AND A PURPOSE BEHIND EVERYTHING THE PRAYER CLUB DOE
HERE'S WHERE THEY FIND GUIDANCE AND MEANING FOR THEIR LIVES:

"GOD DEMONSTRATES HIS OWN LOVE FC
US IN THIS: WHILE WE WERE STILL SINNER
CHRIST DIED FOR US."

Romans 5:8 (New International Versi

"DO NOT LET ANY UNWHOLESOME TALK COME OUT OF YOUR MOUTHS, BUT ONLY WHAT IS HELPFUL FOR BUILDING OTHERS UP ACCORDING TO THEIR NEEDS, THAT IT MAY BENEFIT THOSE WHO LISTEN."

Ephesians 4:29 (NIV)

"JESUS REPLIED, 'MOSES PERMITTED YOU TO DIVORCE YOUR WIVES BECAUSE YOUR HEARTS WERE HARD. BUT IT WAS NOT THIS WAY FROM THE BEGINNING.'"

Matthew 19:8 (NIV

and Verse

"THERE IS NOTHING CONCEALED THAT WILL NOT BE DISCLOSED, OR HIDDEN THAT WILL NOT BE MADE KNOWN."

Matthew 10:26 (NIV)

"ABSTAIN FROM SINFUL DESIRES, WHICH WAR AGAINST YOUR SOUL."

1 Peter 2:11 (NIV)

"HE WHO HAS BEEN STEALING MUST STEAL NO LONGER, BUT MUST WORK, DOING SOMETHING USEFUL WITH HIS OWN HANDS, THAT HE MAY HAVE SOMETHING TO SHARE WITH THOSE IN NEED."

Ephesians 4:28 (NIV)

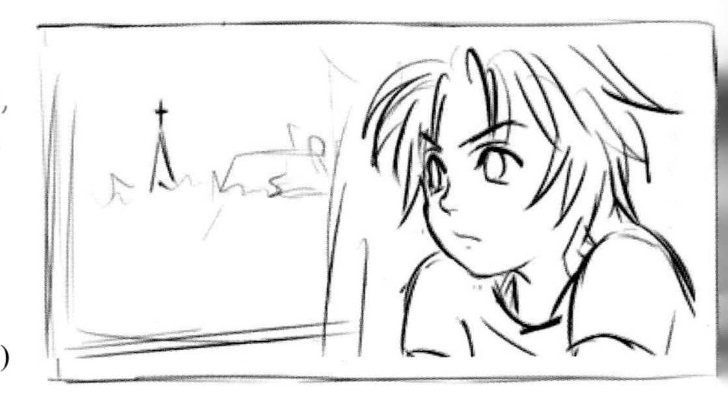

BOTTOM LINE:

"THIS IS LOVE: NOT THAT WE LOVED GOD, BUT THAT HE LOVED US AND SENT HIS SON AS AN ATONING SACRIFICE FOR OUR SINS. DEAR FRIENDS, SINCE GOD SO LOVED US, WE ALSO OUGHT TO LOVE ONE ANOTHER."

1 John 4:10-11 (NIV)

Sign-up for e-mail news at

www.serenitybuzz.com

- **Get downloads**
- **Chat with the author**
- **Preview upcoming books**
- **Meet the characters**

THE PEOPLE BEHIND THE SCENES. . .

BUZZ DIXON is the founder of Realbuzz Studios. A veteran of the comic and cartoon industry, Buzz has worked with Stan Lee of Marvel Comics, and on numerous projects ranging from Precious Moments to Tiny Toons to G. I. Joe. Buzz and his family live in southern California.

MIN "KEIIII" KWON is responsible for penciling and inking Serenity. Although primarily a manga illustrator, the recent Rutgers graduate works in many different forms of visual art.

SERENITY

ART BY MIN KWON

CREATED BY BUZZ DIXON

ORIGINAL CHARACTER DESIGNS

BY DRIGZ ABROT

SERENITY THROWS A BIG WET SLOPPY ONE OUT TO:
ART G., STAN L., DANA M.,
CRISTINA DLS, LINDA B., KIMBERLY B., MICHAEL K.,
BOBBY + HEATHER LEE D., GEOFF S., KATHLEEN W., NATE B.,
'N' THE CCAL, BIOLA, AND HAMPTON'S POSSES.

LUV U GUYZ !!!

ISBN 1-59310-941-5

Published by Barbour Publishing, Inc., P.O. Box 719, Uhrichsville, Ohio 44683
www.barbourbooks.com

"OUR MISSION IS TO PUBLISH AND DISTRIBUTE
INSPIRATIONAL PRODUCTS OFFERING EXCEPTIONAL VALUE
AND BIBLICAL ENCOURAGEMENT TO THE MASSES."

Printed in China.
5 4 3 2 1